# Back to the Cabin

CANYON HEIGHTS

For Jack and Angus
A.B.

# Back to the Cabin

*written and illustrated by*
## ANN BLADES

ORCA BOOK PUBLISHERS

One day in early summer, Mom told the boys, "We're going to the cabin tomorrow."

Jack and Angus looked at each other and groaned. "We don't want to go to the cabin, Mom. There's no TV at the cabin. There's no soccer field there. There are no video games. There's nothing to do!"

Digger hopped into the van and refused to get out.

At five o'clock the next morning, the boys climbed into the van. "We don't want to go to the cabin, Mom," they groaned. "There's no TV at the cabin. There's no soccer field there. There are no video games. There's nothing to do!"

In the dark they drove out of the city, watching the sun rise over the distant mountains. Digger lay on top of the boys and slept.

As they drove through the tunnels of the Fraser Canyon, Jack and Angus called out, "Yale, Sailor Bar, China Bar, Alexandra, Ferrabee, Hells Gate."

"When are we going to get there, Mom?"

They guessed the names of the towns ahead — Cache Creek, Clinton, 70 Mile House, 100 Mile House — and imagined travelling this way on horseback or in a canoe, long before there were roads.

"When are we going to get there, Mom?"

At last they reached the road to the lake. Digger began to bark.

They sped along the dusty dirt road, past wildflowers at the edge of the forest, past the Forest Service campsite and past the cabins called *Bert's Bawg* and *The Loon-E-Bin*.

"We're here, we're here!" shouted the boys.

Everything was the same as they had left it.

Together Mom, Jack and Angus unlocked the padlocks on the cabin, the boat and the outhouse. They unpacked the van and dragged the boat to the lake. They primed the pump.

Beneath the trees the ground was covered with moss, wildflowers and mushrooms. The air was filled with the smells of the forest.

A squirrel chattered at them from a tree branch over the woodpile, and the call of the loons echoed across the lake.

There was lots to do at the cabin.

The boys dragged dead branches and logs to the pit by the lake and built a huge bonfire. They soaked the ground around the pit with buckets of water and threw more and more branches into the flames. Soon the fire roared and sparks flew.

When the branches had burned down to glowing coals, Mom and the boys roasted wieners.

Some afternoons they went fishing. Mom, Jack and Angus rowed to their favourite spot. "We're in the weed zone!" They hooked the worms, dropped their lines and drifted, then rowed back and drifted again.

Loons popped up near the boat. A muskrat paddled around on his back, chewing a weed.

The boys caught lots of fish. They threw all the trout back into the lake except two to fry for breakfast.

One morning Jack and Angus pulled the rotten boards off the old dock with a crowbar and a hammer. Together they rolled the two large logs into the lake and built a new dock.

Then they dropped an anchor off the end of the dock to hold it in place.

The boys explored the crowded dark spaces beneath the cabin. They found a bathtub, sinks, toilets, beds, chairs, tables, windows, doors, bottles, cans, coal, decorations, a broken flashlight, a vacuum cleaner, lots of lumber, firewood, moose antlers and a squirrel's tail.

Anything useful was dragged into the open, and they began work on a fort beside the lake. It would have four sides, a roof and a spy-hole to watch people approaching from the water.

From dawn until dusk the boys swam in the lake. They cannonballed off the dock, screaming as they hit the water. They raced each other on their air mattresses. They fell off the dock into the water fully clothed.

They went swimming when it rained and when it hailed.

But the water was cold. Before long Jack and Angus would run for the cabin, teeth chattering and bodies shaking.

They poured kettles of water into the big green bucket.

"It's my turn first!"

"No fair; you were first last time!"

While one soaked, the other shivered in front of the wood stove and watched the clock. "Your time's up!"

After the bath, the boys filled the kettles and put wood in the stove so there would be warm water next time.

One night Jack and Angus woke to the sound of distant thunder. They lay in bed and counted, "One thousand, two thousand, three thousand," as they watched the lightning through the skylights. They listened while the storm approached the lake and moved across the water until it was right over the cabin. Thunder boomed and lightning flashed above them.

"Will it hit the cabin, Mom?" Rain pounded the roof and drowned their voices.

But slowly the storm passed. Thunder became a distant rumble, the rain a gentle tapping on the roof. The boys fell asleep while Digger stirred and rolled over at the foot of Mom's bed.

On rainy days Jack and Angus built a fire in the big stone fireplace and took turns stoking it. The cabin was filled with the smell of burning wood and the sounds of the crackling fire, the tapping of the rain on the roof and the hissing of the kettles on the wood stove.

Everyone played Monopoly and ate snacks from the green trunk where Mom kept special treats.

Then one day Mom told the boys, "We're going home soon."

The boys looked at each other and groaned. "We don't want to go home, Mom. There's no fishing at home. There's no lake there. There's no boat. There's no fort. There's nothing to do!"

On their last morning at the cabin, Jack and Angus helped load the van. They dragged the boat from the lake and put the padlocks on the cabin, the boat and the outhouse.

Then they took one last look around.

"Maybe next time we'll beat our record of seventeen fish."

"And we can finish the fort."

A squirrel chattered at them from a tree branch over the woodpile, and the call of the loons echoed across the lake.

They'd be back soon.

The publisher would like to acknowledge
the ongoing financial support of the Canada Council,
the Department of Canadian Heritage and the British Columbia
Ministry of Small Business, Tourism and Culture.

Orca Book Publishers          Orca Book Publishers
PO Box 5626, Station B        PO Box 468
Victoria, BC  V8R 6S4         Custer, WA  98240-0468
Canada                        USA

Canadian Cataloguing in Publication Data

Blades, Ann, 1947 –
Back to the cabin

ISBN 1-55143-049-5 (bound)

I.  Title.
PS8553.L33B32 1996    jC813'.54    C96–910283–6
PZ7.B535Ba 1996

Design by Christine Toller
Printed and bound in Hong Kong

10   9   8   7   6   5   4   3   2   1